This Walker book belongs to:

....

....

....

First published individually as:
Bouncing, *Giving*, (1993), *Hiding* and *Chatting* (1994)
by Walker Books Ltd 87 Vauxhall Walk, London SE11 5HJ

This edition published 2017

2 4 6 8 10 9 7 5 3 1

© 1993, 1994, 2015 Shirley Hughes

The right of Shirley Hughes to be identified as author/illustrator
of this work has been asserted by her in accordance with
the Copyright, Designs and Patents Act 1988

This book has been typeset in Sabon

Printed in China

British Library Cataloguing in Publication Data:
a catalogue record for this book is available
from the British Library

ISBN: 978-1-4063-6597-9

www.walker.co.uk

LET'S JOIN IN
A FIRST BOOK OF BEDTIME STORIES

Shirley Hughes

WALKER BOOKS
AND SUBSIDIARIES

LONDON • BOSTON • SYDNEY • AUCKLAND

A Note from Shirley Hughes

In this book, the fun of exploring
'doing words' such as *bouncing*, *hiding*,
chatting or *giving* is captured in four
adventures that a little pre-school heroine
and her baby brother go on during the day.

Small children can absorb these words with
total fascination long before they can read.
They too can join in with Katie and Olly,
by looking at the lively images on the chapter
pages and saying what they have done
during their own busy day.

Shirley Hughes

CONTENTS

Let's join in!

 running

 digging

 hugging

 crawling

 drinking

 counting

 painting

 bending

 stamping

 sitting

 looking

 hiding

 sucking

 sweeping

 sweeping

 reading

 smiling

 bouncing

 scowling

HIDING

You can't see me, I'm hiding!

Here I am.

I'm hiding again! Bet you can't
find me this time!

Under a bush in the garden is
a very good place to hide.
So is a big umbrella,

or down at the
end of the bed.

Sometimes Dad hides
behind a newspaper.

And Mum hides
behind a book
on the sofa.

You can even hide
under a hat.

Tortoises hide inside their shells when they aren't feeling friendly.

And hamsters hide right at the back of their cages when they want to go to sleep.

When the baby hides his eyes he thinks you can't see him. But he's there all the time!

A lot of things
seem to hide –
the moon behind
the clouds ...

and the
sun behind
the trees.

Flowers need to hide in the
ground in wintertime.

But they come peeping out
again in the spring.

Buster always hides when
it's time for his bath,

and so does Mum's purse when
we're all ready to go out shopping.

Our favourite place to hide is behind the kitchen door. Then we jump out – BOO!

And can you guess
who's hiding behind
these curtains?

You're right!
Now we're coming out –
is everyone clapping?

Let's join in!

skipping   telling   listening   waving   dancing

shouting   eating   smelling   chatting   kicking

giving   stroking   thinking   crying   yawning

washing   sleeping   singing   writing   tearing

GIVING

I gave Mum a present on her birthday,
all wrapped up in pretty paper.
And she gave me a big kiss.

I gave Dad a very special picture which I painted at play-group. And he gave me a ride on his shoulders most of the way home.

I gave the baby some slices
of my apple.

We ate them sitting under the table.

At teatime the baby gave me
two of his soggy crusts.

That wasn't much of a present!

You can give someone a
cross look ...

or a big smile!

You can give a tea party ...

or a seat on a crowded bus.

31

On my birthday Grandma and Grandpa
gave me a beautiful doll's pram.
I said "Thank you" and gave
them each a big hug.

And I gave my dear Bemily
a ride in it, all the way
down the garden path
and back again.

I tried to give the cat a
ride too, but she gave me
a nasty scratch!

So Dad had to give
my poor arm a kiss and
a wash and a piece
of sticking plaster.

Sometimes, just when
I've built a big castle
out of bricks,

the baby comes along and
gives it a big swipe!
And it all falls down.

Then I feel like giving
the baby a big
swipe too.

But I don't, because he *is*
my baby brother, after all.

Let's join in!

laughing

aching

pushing

pouring

kissing

sulking

pretending

sneezing

blowing

giving

building

swinging

chatting

resting

catching

dribbling

hammering

hopping

CHATTING

I like chatting.

I chat to the cat,

and I chat in
the car.

I chat with
friends in
the park,

and to the lady at the
supermarket.

Grown-ups like
chatting too.

Sometimes these
chats go on for
rather a long time.

The lady next door is an
especially good chatter.

When Mum is busy she says
that there are just too many
chatterboxes around.

So I go off and
chat to Bemily –
but she never
says a word.

The baby likes
a chat on his toy
telephone. He makes
a lot of calls.

But I can chat to
Grandma and Grandpa
on the real telephone.

Some of the best chats
of all are with Dad, when he
comes to say good night.

Let's join in!

balancing

stretching

cooking

finding

measuring

bouncing

hiding

waiting

pulling

teaching

sliding

climbing

marching

throwing

tasting

standing

tickling

pointing

BOUNCING

When I throw my big shiny ball ...

it bounces away from me.

Bounce, bounce, bounce, bounce!

Then it rolls along the ground, then it stops.

I like bouncing too.

In the mornings I bounce on my bed,
and the baby bounces in his cot.

Mum and Dad's big bed is an
even better place to bounce.

But Dad doesn't much like being
bounced on in the early morning.

So we roll on the floor instead, and
the baby bounces on ME!

After breakfast he
does some dancing
in his baby-bouncer,

and I do some dancing
to the radio.

At my play-group there are big cushions
on the floor where lots of children
can bounce together.

And at home there's
a big sofa where we
can bounce when
Mum isn't looking.

Grandpa and I know a good bouncing game.
I ride on his knees and we sing:

This is the way
the ladies ride:
trit-trot, trit-trot;

This is the way
the gentlemen ride:
tarran, tarran;

This is the way
the farmers ride:
clip-clop, clip-clop;

This is the way
the jockeys ride:
gallopy, gallopy ...

and FALL OFF!

I like bouncing.

I bounce about all day ...

bounce,
bounce,
bounce,
bounce!

Until in the end I stop bouncing,
and go off to sleep.